Kids Love Reading
Choose Your Own Adventure®!

"I liked this book, but it's not safe to build your own robot!"
Jake Buckingham, age 7

"I like Choose Your Own Adventure more than normal books.
In a normal book I would have read two or three chapters
but instead I read three stories."
Soren Bay-Hansen, age 7

"This book was good. I like that I got to pick how the story went."
Lily Von Trapp, age 7

"This book was funny, whoa!"
Anna Kenyon, age 7

"I thought the robot was funny and nice. If I built a robot
I would make him read to me and do my homework."
Azailea Morales, age 8

"Sometimes it's a hard choice, but I still like that I get to choose."
Liam Stewart, age 6

Illustrated by: Keith Newton
Book and cover design by: Stacey Boyd, Big Eyedea Visual Design

For information regarding permission, write to:

CHOOSECO

P.O. Box 46
Waitsfield, Vermont 05673
www.cyoa.com

A DRAGONLARK BOOK

ISBN: 1-937133-44-3
EAN: 978-1-937133-44-3

Published simultaneously in the United States and Canada

Printed in China

0 9 8 7 6 5 4 3 2 1

CHOOSE YOUR OWN ADVENTURE®

GUS VS. THE ROBOT KING

BY R. A. MONTGOMERY
AND SHANNON GILLIGAN

ILLUSTRATED BY KEITH NEWTON

A DRAGONLARK BOOK

To David Curtis, with Love.

READ THIS FIRST!!!

WATCH OUT!
THIS BOOK IS DIFFERENT
from *every* book you've ever read.

Do not read this book from the first page
through to the last page.
Instead, start on page 1 and read until you
come to your first choice. Then turn to the
page shown and see what happens.

When you come to the end of a story,
you can go back and start again.
Every choice leads to a new adventure.

Good luck!

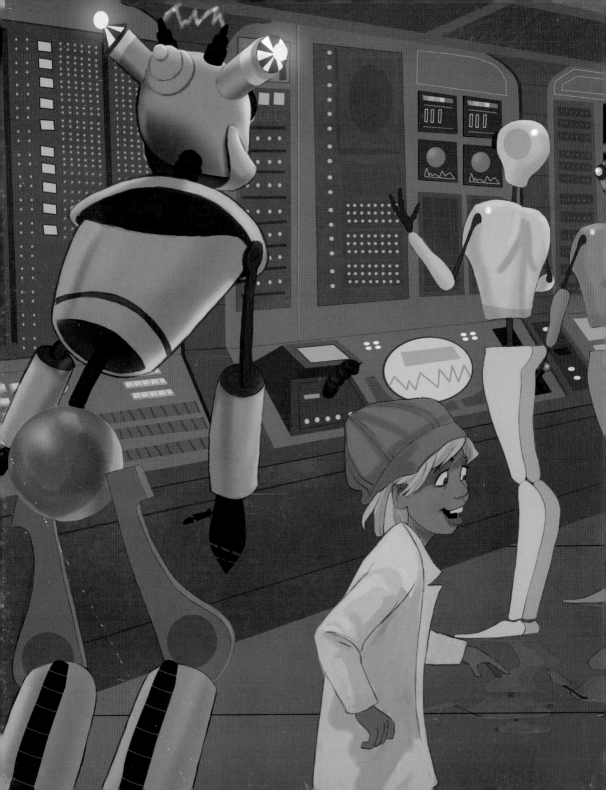

Gus is your very own robot and good friend. A few years ago, you built Gus out of left-over robot parts from your parents' lab. They were proud of you, but WORRIED. Gus is a handful. Your dad said, "Nobody really knows what the future of robots will be. They become more like humans all the time. Be careful. Gus might not always do what you say."

Turn to page 2.

"Mom," you ask, "why does Dad dislike Gus?"

"Oh, he doesn't dislike Gus. He's just worried about artificial intelligence," your Mom says. "Every year robots are getting smarter and smarter."

"But Mom, how can Gus get smarter? I built him several years ago," you say.

"We don't really understand," your mom replies. "But something is going on. There are even rumors that there is a King of Robots who wants to take over the world."

"Mom, that's silly," you say. "Robots can't take over."

Turn to page 4.

You leave the kitchen and head to the garage where Gus lives. He likes it there. He has a slot next to the tool bench, above the oil cans. If there is one thing about Gus, he loves to tinker with tools. Your dad is right. Gus is one smart robot!

"Yah-Mon!" Gus says, trying to sound like a reggae singer. "What's happening?"

Turn to page 6.

"Gus, we have a little problem," you say.

"Is it the anchovies in the vanilla ice cream? I thought your dad might not like that."

"Well, he didn't love it. But it's not that," you answer. "Have you heard anything about the King of Robots?"

Go on to the next page.

"Yes," Gus says. Suddenly all his lights start to blink. "I've heard of the King." He sounds different.

"Gus," you whisper, "is the King of Robots good or is he bad?"

Gus's lights continue to blink wildly. He shakes his arms and nods his head. He sounds funny when he says, "Hard-to-say… He-asked-me-to-join-him-and-his-band-of-super-robots…I-am-a-bit-afraid-to-go-alone… Would-you-like-to-come-with-me?"

You have never heard Gus speak like this.

If you convince Gus to wait until you can find out more about the King of Robots from your good friend Schuyler, turn to page 8.

If you decide to go with Gus to meet the King of Robots, turn to page 15.

"Gus," you say, "there is something I've got to tell you. And you won't like it."

"What? What?" Gus replies. He sounds like himself again. No more robot-speak.

"I think we should go ask Schuyler about the King of Robots. Just to be safe," you say.

Gus makes a robot frown. He doesn't get along with Schuyler. "Oh, all right."

Turn to page 10.

"Let's go find Officer Paddy and report this to him," you suggest. Officer Paddy is the sheriff for your neighborhood.

"He'll be at the Slurp Shop getting his daily root beer float," Gus adds.

You find Paddy a few minutes later.

"Hey kids, what's up?" he asks.

"There's going to be a robot riot down at the docks," Gus says.

"Now, look, don't you worry. I think robots should have some rights. Don't you agree, Gus?" Paddy replies.

His walkie-talkie squawks before you can answer.

Turn to page 18.

You and Gus walk three doors up the street and knock. Schuyler answers her front door.

"Hey! I was just going to come find you two. I've got news. The King of Robots is calling a meeting of all the robots in town. They say he wants to take over City Hall. He wants to be mayor. Then he wants to run for Congress. And then he wants to be president. Maybe."

Turn to page 12.

"Where did you hear this?" you ask.

"I found it on RobotNews.com, the secret robot news website. It was the headline," Schuyler replies. She turns to Gus. "Is it true? The meeting starts in 15 minutes. It's downtown at the docks."

That's smart, you think. There are so many robots loading and unloading the big ships at the docks. Who will notice a few extra robots having a meeting?

If you decide to warn the police about the robot meeting, turn to page 9.

If you decide to dress up as robots, and attend the King of Robot's meeting with Gus, turn to page 20.

You and Gus head downtown to the Robot Association offices. You notice a big banner hanging from the building. It says:

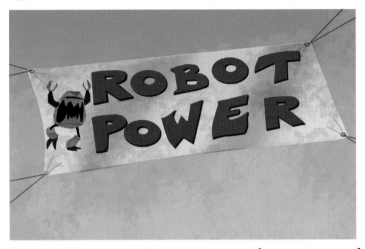

As you try to go in, two robot guards stop you.

"Humans are not allowed inside," one says, pointing at you.

"Says who?" Gus demands.

"Says the King," the other robot says.

"Well, tell the King his cousin Gus is here," Gus says.

Turn to page 26.

Gus runs out the front door and down the walk.

"Gus, slow down," you yell, running. You catch up about half a block down the street.

"Gus, how do you know the Robot King anyway?" you ask.

"I'm not sure I should tell," Gus answers.

You stop. "Gus! Remember what my mom and dad said about telling the truth?"

Gus looks down at his robot shoes. "Yes," he says quietly. "I remember. Always tell the truth. Especially when it can get you in trouble."

You have to laugh. "Well, that's not exactly what they said. It's more like…"

"The kind of stuff we lie about is the stuff that gets us into trouble," Gus says. "I know."

"Exactly," you say. "So how do you know the Robot King?"

Turn to page 16.

"Okay, I'll tell the truth. He's my cousin. We met on Planet Argos. And I invited him to visit Planet Earth," Gus explains.

"When did you go to Planet Argos?"

"During your last summer vacation," Gus says. "You got to visit the Grand Canyon with your parents and I was supposed to stay all by myself on a shelf in the garage?"

"Where is the Robot King now?" you ask.

"He's probably downtown at the Robot Association. Either there or at the docks giving a speech about Robot Rights," Gus explains.

If you decide to go looking for the Robot King downtown, turn to page 13.

If you decide to head to the docks to find the Robot King, turn to page 37.

"Captain, where would you like to go?" a small voice says. It's coming from a cup holder! You move closer and see a small robot the size of a candy bar smiling at you.

"You can fly this thing?" Schuyler asks.

There is a loud THUMP on the hatch from outside. You need to decide quickly.

If you tell the mini-robot to take you to the Robot King, turn to page 41.

If you decide to go to Tarsa, a planet famous for robot studies, turn to page 44.

"ALERT! DISTURBANCE AT THE DOCKS! ROBOTS HIJACK FREIGHTER! ALERT! ALL DUTY OFFICERS REPORT TO DOCKS AREA IMMEDIATELY."

"We better go!" you shout to Paddy.

You all leap onto his motorcycle—*Vroom! Vroom!*—and off you zoom.

You pull up to the docks. There's a stand-off between the cops and the robots. Paddy's Sergeant runs up. "They are threatening to sink the ship. It's filled with chocolate sauce, peppermint bits, honey, and three kinds of nuts. That ship sinks and there will be no hot fudge sundaes for months. We want to negotiate, but they are talking in a robot language. It sounds like a bunch of crickets! Nobody can understand a thing!"

"Oh, I speak Cricket," Gus says. "Maybe I can translate?"

Go on to the next page.

You're not sure how or where Gus learned to speak Cricket, but Gus saves the day. He helps the police negotiate with the robots who have hijacked the chocolate freighter. The robots give the ship back. The mayor agrees to have a hearing to listen to the robots' problems.

"I want to apologize to everyone," the Robot King states. "And three cheers for Gus, who helped everyone get along."

Hip-hip-hooray!

Hip-hip-hooray!

Hip-hip-hooray!

The End

You and Schuyler and Gus run home to your parents' workshop and attach some old robot parts to your arms and legs. You also find two small garbage cans, which you turn into robot heads.

Gus laughs. "You are definitely low-cost robots!"

"Quoot laaffing oor wee woon't bringgg you aloongg," you tell him. The garbage can head makes your voice sound funny.

"Lead us to the docks," Schuyler orders Gus. "I can't see a thing inside this garbage can headpiece."

"Follow me this way," Gus says. He takes your hands and leads you both down the street to wait for the Robot Bus.

Turn to page 23.

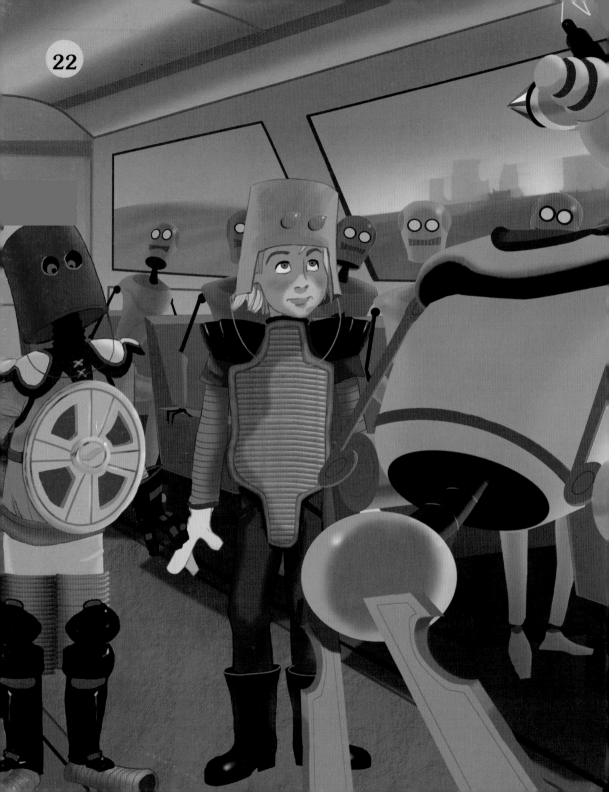

You, Schuyler and Gus wait a few minutes and the Robot Bus arrives. You climb aboard. The Robot Bus driver puts his bus on automatic while the he comes down the aisle punching tickets.

"Ticket?" he asks you.

"Wee doon't haff any tickets," you tell him through your garbage can head.

Turn to page 25.

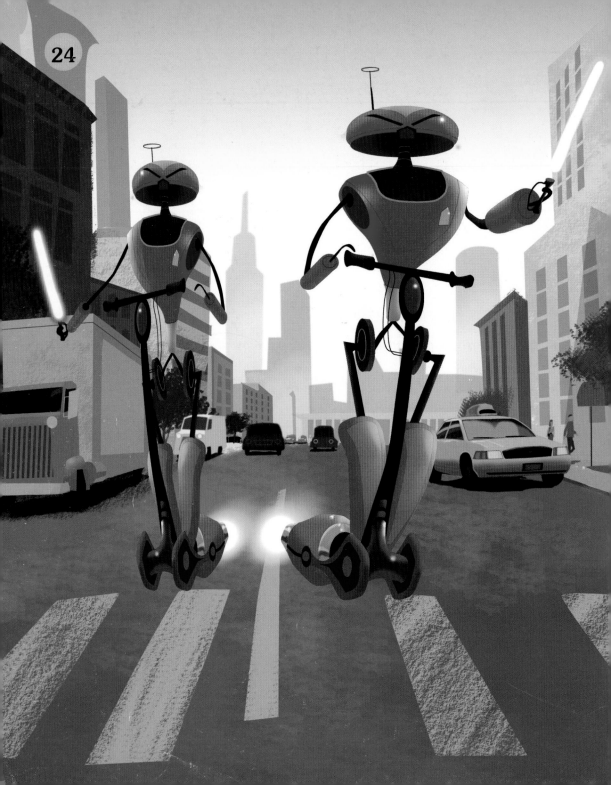

He talks into a small microphone attached to his shoulder.

"Two unidentified passengers aboard Bus #16. Repeat. Two passenger attempting to ride Robot Bus #16 with NO TICKETS. Prepare to intercept," he says.

You look ahead and spot two red security robots running down the street toward your bus. They carry electronic wands.

If you stay where you are, turn to page 48.

If you decide to run for it, turn to page 68.

"Cousin? Okay. You should have said so," the first robot guard says. "Go on in."

Gus leads the way. Inside it looks more like a lab than an office. And the lab is filled with tanks of jellyfish.

"Gus, what are all the jellyfish for?" you whisper.

"For brains," he whispers.

"What do you mean brains?" you ask. "What kind of brains? Why do you need them?"

Turn to page 29.

"For him," Gus says, pointing to a desk at the far end of the lab. "And for all the other robots who want super brain power."

"Gus!" a voice bellows. "Good to see you!"

It's the Robot King. He's sitting at his desk. But his head is detached from his body. It's sitting on the desk talking to you.

If you decide it's too scary and you want to leave right now, turn to page 32.

If you decide to ask Gus why the jellyfish can give robots special brain power, turn to page 36.

"The saucer! Follow me!" Gus yells. He runs toward the flying saucer and disappears inside. You and Schuyler run after him. You hear the insect robot's antennae snapping at your feet as you pull the hatch shut.

The saucer is dim inside. There is a large bank of blinking lights. It must be the drive control panel. You notice seven cup holders evenly spaced along its rim.

Turn to page 17.

You decide you want to leave. "The Robot King without a head is too scary," you tell Gus.

"Okay," he agrees. "You're the boss. Where to next?"

"How about a hot fudge sundae at the Slurp Shop," you suggest. "I'll treat."

Gus grins from ear to ear.

The End.

"Let's run for the hills," you cry. You, Gus, and Schuyler run to the door marked EXIT.

"It's locked!" Schuyler cries.

You can hear the insect robot rasping its feelers behind you.

"I don't like this one teeny bit," Schuyler says.

"Please-show-me-your-identification-now," the insect robot demands.

Gus shows the insect robot the three copper disks for getting back stage to meet the Robot King.

The insect extends one of his six legs and grabs the disks from Gus.

"This-way-please," he says, skittering off to a door on the other side of the hangar.

Turn to page 35.

You, Gus and Schuyler follow his orders. The room is a dusty old storeroom filled with strange airplane parts.

"Stay here," the insect commands.

He shuts the door and locks it. The three of you wait all morning. At first there is lots of noise in the hangar. You hear the rocket ships take off. Then everything goes quiet.

"Did they forget about us?" you wonder.

"Help!" the three of you yell. "Help!" But no one answers. Finally, around lunchtime, someone unlocks the door.

"Dad! Mom!" you cry. "You found us!"

"Thanks to the electronic finder button we installed in Gus," your mom says. "But how did you end up here?"

You look at Gus and Schuyler. "Long story. Can we eat lunch first? We're starving."

The End

"How do the jellyfish give robots brain power?" you ask. The Robot King looks scary without a head attached.

"It's easy. You plug a jellyfish into a robot command processor. We use the jellyfish to think new thoughts," Gus explains. "Jellyfish have very specialized nervous systems. Remember that robots are just programmed to do things. They aren't programmed to think like..." Gus stops mid-sentence. All his lights start blinking wildly. "I-cannot-tell-you-anymore," he says. "I-am-loyal-to-the-Robot-King."

"Okay Gus our friendship is over," you announce. "If you won't tell me the truth we can't be friends."

"Nononono! I am here to be your friend. You made me! We are a great success together!" Gus whispers. He pauses. "I too use a jellyfish to help me think."

Turn to page 38.